Around the World in Eighty Days

JULES VERNE

Saddleback's *Illustrated Classics*™

ISBN-13: 978-1-56254-882-7
ISBN-10: 1-562-54882-4
eBook: 978-1-60291-140-6

Printed in Guangzhou, China
1109/11-68-09

15 14 13 12 11 10 09   2 3 4 5 6 7 8

Welcome to
Saddleback's *Illustrated Classics*™

We are proud to welcome you to Saddleback's *Illustrated Classics*™. Saddleback's *Illustrated Classics*™ was designed specifically for the classroom to introduce readers to many of the great classics in literature. Each text, written and adapted by teachers and researchers, has been edited using the Dale-Chall vocabulary system. In addition, much time and effort has been spent to ensure that these high-interest stories retain all of the excitement, intrigue, and adventure of the original books.

With these graphically *Illustrated Classics*™, you learn what happens in the story in a number of different ways. One way is by reading the words a character says. Another way is by looking at the drawings of the character. The artist can tell you what kind of person a character is and what he or she is thinking or feeling.

This series will help you to develop confidence and a sense of accomplishment as you finish each novel. The stories in Saddleback's *Illustrated Classics*™ are fun to read. And remember, fun motivates!

Overview

Everyone deserves to read the best literature our language has to offer. Saddleback's *Illustrated Classics*™ was designed to acquaint readers with the most famous stories from the world's greatest authors, while teaching essential skills. You will learn how to:

- Establish a purpose for reading
- Use prior knowledge
- Evaluate your reading
- Listen to the language as it is written
- Extend literary and language appreciation through discussion and writing activities

Reading is one of the most important skills you will ever learn. It provides the key to all kinds of information. By reading the *Illustrated Classics*™ , you will develop confidence and the self-satisfaction that comes from accomplishment— a solid foundation for any reader.

Step-By-Step

The following is a simple guide to using and enjoying each of your *Illustrated Classics*™. To maximize your use of the learning activities provided, we suggest that you follow these steps:

1. ***Listen!*** We suggest that you listen to the read-along. (At this time, please ignore the beeps.) You will enjoy this wonderfully dramatized presentation.

2. ***Pre-reading Activities.*** After listening to the audio presentation, the pre-reading activities in the Activity Book prepare you for reading the story by setting the scene, introducing more difficult vocabulary words, and providing some short exercises.

3. ***Reading Activities.*** Now turn to the "While you are reading" portion of the Activity Book, which directs you to make a list of story-related facts. Read-along while listening to the audio presentation. (This time pay attention to the beeps, as they indicate when each page should be turned.)

4. ***Post-reading Activities.*** You have successfully read the story and listened to the audio presentation. Now answer the multiple-choice questions and other activities in the Activity Book.

Remember,

"Today's readers are tomorrow's leaders."

Jules Verne

Jules Verne, a French novelist, was born in France in 1828. He studied law but instead became one of the very first science fiction writers.

The popular interest in science in the 1800s led Verne to write very realistic and detailed stories that used science and technology. In these stories he wrote about such modern things as airplanes, submarines, television, guided missiles, and space satellites *before* they were even invented. His detailed descriptions of these items even accurately predicted their real uses. The *Nautilus,* the submarine that he wrote about in *Twenty Thousand Leagues Under the Sea* and which also appears in *The Mysterious Island,* was written about twenty-five years before the first successful power submarine was invented.

Verne also knew a great deal about geography and used this knowledge to make his stories of travel and adventure seem quite real. In *Around the World in Eighty Days* the main character Phileas Fogg, on a bet, makes a trip around the world in the then unheard of time of eighty days. The realistic geographical descriptions of this daring feat made the book one of Verne's most popular works.

Jules Verne died in 1905.

Saddleback's *Illustrated Classics*™

Around the World in Eighty Days

JULES VERNE

THE MAIN CHARACTERS

Phileas Fogg

Passepartout

Detective Fix

Aouda

In 1872, Mr. Phileas Fogg lived at No. 7 Savile Row in London's wealthy Burlington Gardens. Little was known about him except that he was a man of the world.

He was one of the most noted members of the Reform Club, though he did not work for a living and always tried to avoid calling attention to himself.

Was Phileas Fogg rich? He must have been! But those who knew him best could not imagine how he had made his fortune.

For years he had passed every single day from 11:30 A.M. to exactly 12:00 midnight at the club. He talked very little, and all he ever did there was read the paper and play cards.

He often won at cards, which pleased him very much.

His winnings he kept in a special fund for charity. Mr. Fogg played not to win, but just for the fun of playing.

He always ate breakfast and dinner at the club and always used the same room. He ate at the same times every day, always alone.

When he dined, all the cooks of the club's kitchen worked together to crowd his table with their finest food and drink.

If to live in this style seems strange to others, then there certainly must be some good in being strange.

Though at home only a few hours each day, Mr. Fogg wanted his only servant to be perfect. On the second of October, for example, he had fired one man for bringing his shaving water at eighty-four degrees instead of eighty-six. Then he looked about for someone else.

The new servant!

You are a French-man, and your name is John?

Jean, if you please. Jean Passe-partout. It is a name that was given to me because of many different jobs. I have been a singer, a circus rider, a tightrope walker, a teacher of gymnastics, and a fireman in Paris.

But hearing that Monsieur Phileas Fogg was the most exact of gentlemen in England, I have come to find a peaceful life of service.

The name Passepartout suits me, and you are well spoken of. You know what you must do?

Yes, monsieur.

Good! From this moment, twenty-six minutes after eleven A. M., this second day of October, you are in my service.

That morning, as on every other, Mr. Phileas Fogg placed his right foot in front of his left foot 575 times and reached the Reform Club at the usual hour.

He passed the day just as he did all others.

That evening he was joined by his usual partners for cards. They were all rich and well known, even in a club for only the princes of English money.

It included Gauthier Ralph, one of the directors of the Bank of England.

Well, Ralph, what about the robbery?

We'll catch him. I have detectives watching every port.

But do they know what to look for?

The Daily Telegram says he's a gentleman.

The robbery was the talk of the town. A package of notes worth 55,000 pounds had been taken from the Bank of England. The daring thief had simply picked them up from a table and walked off.

The card game began, but between hands, talk of the robbery started up again.

I say that the chances are in the robber's favor. The world is a big place.

It was once. Cut the cards, sir.

Again there was quiet as the hand was played.

Well now, just because you can go 'round the world in three months...

Correction: in eighty days!

That is true, as the Daily Telegram says, now that the Great Indian Railroad is open.

But what of bad weather, train wrecks and such?

It's still eighty days.

I'd bet that can't be done!

Very well. I have 20,000 pounds at Barings which I will bet.

You are joking! 20,000 pounds which could be lost by a single delay?

A true Englishman does not joke about a bet.

I will bet I can circle the world in eighty days or less. Do you accept?

After talking together, his partners answered:

We accept!

Good! The train leaves for Dover at a quarter to nine. I will take it.

The group offered to stop the game so Mr. Fogg could get ready to leave.

I am ready enough now, thank you. Let us finish the game, gentlemen.

And so, twenty minutes later, having won twenty guineas at cards, Mr. Fogg left the Reform Club to travel around the world.

Monsieur, you are not due back here until midnight!

I know, but we are going 'round the world! I must find my passport.

Get a suitcase with two shirts and three pairs of socks for me and the same for you. Hurry up!

Take good care of this bag. There are 20,000 pounds in it.

They got to the station at twenty past eight, and Phileas Fogg reached for the twenty guineas he had just won at cards.

RAILROAD STATION

Here, my good woman. I'm glad I met you.

Well, gentlemen, I'll see you at quarter to nine on Saturday, the twenty-first of December.

Then Phileas Fogg and his servant boarded the train. Moments later it glided from the station.

Six days later, two men waited at the Suez Canal for the ship Mongolia. It had come from Italy and was on its way to India.

But really, Detective Fix, I don't see how you'll know the robber even if he is on board.

I have a feeling about these things, Consul. If he's on board, he won't slip through my fingers!

When the boat arrived, Fix stood where he could see all the passengers.

Soon...

I need to have this checked. Can you show me to the consul?

Fix was quite surprised. The wording on this man's passport was the same as that sent to him by Scotland Yard for the bank robber.

Is this your passport?

No, it's my master's.

He must go in person to the consul.

Very well. I will go and get him.

I must keep him here until I get a warrant from London. I hope you will not let him go.

Ah, that's your problem. If it is a good passport, I have no right to refuse.

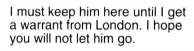

But as he spoke, a knock was heard at the door.

Very good, sir but you do not need my stamp to go to India.

I know, but I wish to prove that I came by way of the Suez.

I'll agree that he looks right, but...

I'll make sure of it.

Well my friend, having a good trip?

Yes, but we travel so fast it seems more like a dream.

Are you in a hurry, then?

My master is. By the way, I must buy some clothes. We came away without much.

Come, I'll show you a good shop. But tell me, where are you going?

He says we're going around the world on a bet.

So your Mr. Fogg is a strange man, is he?

I should say so.

Is he rich?

Oh, yes, for he has a lot of new banknotes with him.

These answers made the excited detective even more so. Fogg had left England with a large sum of cash soon after the robbery. His story about traveling on a bet could never be true!

I agree that you have a good case against this man. But what can you do?

I'll wire London for a warrant of arrest to be sent to India. Then I'll go aboard the Mongolia, follow the man there and arrest him.

So, after a quick visit to the telegraph office, Fix went aboard the Mongolia and was soon sailing on the waters of the Red Sea.

They sailed past the great cities of the Red Sea, but Phileas Fogg seldom went on deck to see them.

True to his habits, he ate grand meals and played cards constantly. He had found partners as eager as himself to start a good game.

Ah, my kind friend from Suez?

Yes, good to see you again.

Where are you traveling?

Like you, to India. I am an agent of the ship company.

After this meeting, Passepartout got in the habit of talking with Fix, who often bought him a drink at the bar. This made Passepartout think Fix must be a good fellow indeed.

With good weather and all sails aiding the engine, the Mongolia arrived in India two days early.

Until that time, India could only be crossed on foot or horseback. But with the new railroad, a crossing of three days was planned.

They docked at 4:30 P.M. At exactly 8:00 P.M., the train was to leave for Calcutta.

Fix was disappointed to find that the warrant had not arrived. He still could not arrest Fogg.

Meanwhile, Passepartout, having bought the shoes and shirts they needed, took a walk through the streets.

But he walked further than he had meant to go.

No one but Indians could enter certain temples. And when they did, they had to take off their shoes. Three priests quickly grabbed Passepartout and tore off his shoes when he tried to go inside.

But the Frenchman got away. Reaching the station just in time, he told his story in a few words.

I hope that it will not happen again!

With this news, Fix, who was ready to follow them, got a new idea.

On board Fogg and Passepartout met Sir Francis Cromarty, one of Fogg's card partners from the Mongolia.

Sir Francis could not help thinking that this strange gentleman who traveled the world on a bet would leave it without doing any real good.

As they slept, the train passed cotton, coffee, nutmeg, clove, and pepper plantations. Its steam curled in circles around beautiful temples.

When they stopped for breakfast, Passepartout was able to buy some Indian slippers which he wore with great delight.

For two days they went whirling across India at full speed.

But then:

Passengers will get out here.

But the papers said the railroad was completed!

The papers were wrong. There are still fifty miles to go.

Sir Francis, we will look about for some other way to reach our goal.

An elephant was found. When its greedy owner refused to rent his elephant, Mr. Fogg offered to buy it for 1,000 pounds.

24

Perhaps thinking he could make even more money, the man still refused.

I beg you, sir, to think what you are paying here!

A bet of 20,000 pounds is at stake. We need this elephant!

At 2,000 pounds, the Indian gave in.

Good heavens! What a price for an elephant!

A young Parsee was found and was hired to guide them.

And soon they started off through the jungle towards the city.

For almost two days they traveled through Bundelcund. In this place lived people who kept to their old tribal ways.

A group of Brahmins. They must not see us.

That's Kali, the goddess of love and death!

That ugly old woman? The goddess of death, maybe, but love? Never!

Then there followed a beautiful young girl.

She'll be burned at dawn with the body of her husband.

Does she want to do this awful thing?

No. This woman is a Parsee like myself. She does not go willingly.

Indeed, this girl, a beauty of the Parsee tribe, was married against her will to an old rajah of Bundelcund. Her name was Aouda.

I have twelve hours to spare. Suppose we save this woman?

Why, you are a man of heart!

Sometimes, when I have the time.

When evening came, the guide led them to a temple.

It's only eight. Perhaps the guards will become sleepy.

Perhaps.

They waited until midnight, but the guards were still awake.

Be still. We may get our chance at the last moment!

Then Passepartout thought of a plan.

What a silly idea!

The hour arrived. The girl, who had been drugged, was placed beside her dead husband.
A torch was brought.

Look!

Suddenly a cry went through the crowd. Passepartout, dressed as the rajah, rose with the woman in his arms.

Let us be off!

So the job was done, and the fair Aouda was rescued.

28

They finally reached the next city on their journey.

The elephant is yours!

But, sir, he is worth a fortune!

Take him, guide, and I shall still be grateful to you.

Then they turned their attention to Aouda. When they learned that she spoke English, Sir Francis told her what had happened. Fogg said nothing, and Passepartout only blushed.

Learning that she had an uncle in Hong Kong, Fogg offered to bring her there since it was on his way. She was happy to accept this offer.

At Benares, the next city, Sir Francis left them.

That night they crossed the jungle, and at seven the next morning they arrived in Calcutta.

Mr. Phileas Fogg?

Yes.

Please follow me with your servant. I am a policeman.

But the ship leaves at noon.

We shall be on it.

Passepartout must spend fifteen days in jail and must pay a fine of 300 pounds. His master, Mr. Phileas Fogg, must spend a week in jail.

The detective, Fix, still without a warrant, had promised the priests money for damages. He had brought them by train to Calcutta.

A week would be plenty of time for Fix's warrant to arrive. But Fogg knew what he had to do.

I offer bail.

You have that right. Bail is set at 1,000 pounds each.

Ah, these are good shoes.

I will pay at once.

That man is giving up 2,000 pounds. But I'll follow him to the end of the world if I have to!

During the first few days of the journey, Aouda learned more about Fogg.

She looked at him often, but he seemed not to notice it.

Fix got aboard the ship. But a couple of days later, his luck ran against him.

Passepartout wondered why this man kept turning up where they were.

Why, Mr. Fix! Are you with us again?

Er...yes, more company business.

He must be a spy from the Reform Club.

Are you going 'round the world too?

Heavens, no! I must work for a living.

Oh, I'm quite sure of that!

Now Fix was puzzled. He was sure the servant suspected something. But what? And what had he told his master?

Phileas Fogg, however, took no notice of anything but his card game.

During the last days of their voyage, a storm blew up.

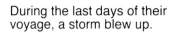

Forced to go slowly, the ship was twenty-four hours late at Hong Kong.

Have you news of the ship Carnatic?

She was delayed by engine trouble and won't sail until tomorrow morning.

But once in Hong Kong, they could not find Aouda's uncle.

He is well known here, but has moved with his family to Holland.

What should I do, Mr. Fogg?

It is very simple. Go on to Europe.

So Passepartout happily went to arrange for three cabins.

But as he neared the ticket office, he met Detective Fix again.

Ah, Mr. Fix! I knew you couldn't be far away!

Er... yes.

So they got cabins for four and learned the ship would sail that very evening.

I must speak with you. Let's drink some wine.

Well, I must not be long.

Fix took Passepartout to an opium den where he first ordered a glass of wine.

I am a detective. I have tracked Mr. Fogg here, yet without a warrant I can do nothing. Help me and I'll share the reward offered by the Bank of England.

Passepartout tried to rise. But, affected by the wine, he fell back in his chair.

Even if what you say were true, he is a good man, and I could never do that.

Very well. Forget I said it. Try some of this.

So saying, he offered Passepartout a pipe of opium.

Now Mr. Fogg will be delayed for sure.

The next morning Mr. Fogg expected to find the ship and his missing servant at the dock.

Excuse me, did you intend to sail on the Carnatic?

Yes, sir.

So did I, but it was repaired early and sailed last night. I am very sorry to miss it.

Detective Fix was certain that he would receive his warrant soon.

There are other ships in Hong Kong, it seems to me.

Is your ship ready to sail?

Yes, it is. The Tankadere is the fastest ship in the harbor.

I must get to Yokohama to catch a ship to San Francisco. I offer 100 pounds a day and a 200-pound bonus if we make it.

We cannot do that. There might be another way.

How?

The San Francisco ship starts from Shanghai, China in four days. With luck we could make it there.

They planned to sail in an hour.

And if you would like to join us...

Thank you, sir. It is very kind of you to offer.

Leaving some money with the police to search for Passepartout, they set sail.

The waters near China were stormy at that time of the year. Even the voyage to Shanghai was risky.

But Captain John Bunsby believed in the Tankadere which rode on the waves like a seagull. He was not wrong.

The voyage went well.
But Fix was troubled by traveling at Mr. Fogg's expense. Still, he had to eat, and so he ate.

I must ask to pay my share!

Let us not even speak of it!

They made good time for two days, and it seemed that Mr. Fogg would easily reach his ship. But there was another problem.

I fear a typhoon is coming up from the south.

Fine. It will carry us forward.

Twenty times the Tankadere seemed almost to be sunk by mountains of water. But each time the captain's skillful hand saved her.

In the morning, when the storm was over, they were within a hundred miles of Shanghai.

But that evening...

What's happening? Your ship is leaving port already!

Signal her!

But where was Passepartout? Three hours after Fix had left him, he woke up.

I must get to the Carnatic!

He had only a few steps to go, and soon reached the ship.

The next day, the sea air cleared his head.

Am I on the Carnatic?

Of course. We are on the way to Yokohama.

When he remembered the sailing time had been changed, he became very upset.

He was on the way to Japan— alone.

He ate enough for three people.

Finally he reached Japan and went ashore.

For a day he wandered from rich shops...

...to the fields of rice.

The next morning he found a dealer who liked his European clothes. He made a good trade for them.

I will make believe I am at a carnival.

And after some breakfast, he made a lucky find.

ACROBATIC TROUPE HONORABLE WILLIAM BATULCAR, PROPRIETOR LAST SHOWS BEFORE DEPARTURE TO THE UNITED STATES LONG NOSES! LONG NOSES!

The United States! That's just what I want!

Would you like a servant, sir?

A servant! I already have two who are very good. They serve me for only their food.

Here they are. But can you sing standing on your head? With a sword balanced on one foot and a spinning top on the other?

Humph! I think so!

And so he joined the company of jugglers. He was soon dressed in another costume.

Now, as you may have guessed, Mr. Fogg managed to get aboard the Yokohama ship. In Yokohama he learned that Passepartout had arrived on the Carnatic. So he and Aouda wandered the streets looking for him. By chance they came to Mr. Batulcar's theater.

Master, my master!

Come, young man. We must get to the ship!

And so, at half past six they stepped aboard the American ship for San Francisco.

When Passepartout learned of their adventures with Mr. Fix, he said nothing. He thought the time had not yet come to tell what had happened between the detective and himself.

On the ninth day of the trip, they had come exactly half way around the globe.

Fifty-two of the eighty days were gone, but because of the route, they had actually covered over two-thirds of the whole journey.

42

And where was Fix? In Yokohama he finally got his warrant, which was now useless since Fogg had left English soil.

Darn! I'll have to follow him across America and the Atlantic Ocean now.

But that very day he met Passpartout who gave him quite a beating.

Stop! Stop!

You deserved that!

I know. But listen. I have been Mr. Fogg's enemy, now I am his friend.

You are sure he is honest?

No. But Mr. Fogg is going back to England. I will follow him, but I will not try to stop him.

Are we friends?

Friends? No, but we can work together. At the least sign of a trick, I'll wring your neck!

So, on the morning of December third, they passed the Golden Gate. They reached San Francisco just on time.

Learning that the train would leave at six that evening, Passepartout was sent shopping. Mr. Fogg and Aouda set off for a walk on the streets of San Francisco. There they met Fix.

What? Have we crossed the Pacific together and not met?

The honor is mine.

Business calls me back to Europe. Are you taking the train this evening, too? I would be happy to travel in such good company.

So they went off to see the sights.

They soon found themselves on Montgomery Street where a great crowd was gathering.

Perhaps we'd better not stay here.

Yes. There may be fighting.

But as they tried to leave, Fix was punched.

You Yankee!

Then they were separated by the crowd.

Englishman, we shall meet again!

As you wish, sir.

Thanks!

No thanks are needed. But a tailor might help.

Their clothing had been torn badly in the fight.

There seems to have been a fight today!

That? Oh, no, sir. It was just a meeting to elect a justice of the peace.

The railroad track which connects San Francisco with New York runs for 3,786 miles.

A crossing of seven days would help Phileas Fogg to take the fast Atlantic ship from New York to Liverpool on December eleventh.

At eight each evening, carefully packed beds were rolled out.
By such a system, each traveler soon had his own comfortable bed.

On the great plains of eastern Nevada they found buffalo.

What a country! Cattle stop the trains!

The parade of buffalo lasted three full hours, but the engineer chose to wait until they were gone. He made up the lost time when the tracks were clear.

Entering Utah, a Mormon elder named William Hitch talked about the Latter Day Saints who had settled the place.

But the elder's story grew too long, and his audience grew less.

Driven from Vermont, Illinois, and Ohio, we have found this land on which to place our tents. Will you not place yours here too, under our flag?

No! I must finish my trip 'round the world!

In Ogden, Utah, the train rested for six hours. Mr. Fogg and his group had time to visit Salt Lake City.

In this strange country, everything is done in squares: the cities, the houses, and even the fun.

Soon they crossed the Rocky Mountains.

Why did my master choose winter? Couldn't he have waited for a warmer season?

They stopped in Green River, Wyoming.

The man from the meeting in San Francisco. Mr. Fogg must not see him!

Aouda found a moment when Mr. Fogg slept to tell what she had seen.

A meeting between them might spoil everything!

We must keep him from leaving the car and hope that luck is with us.

Were you not in the habit of playing cards on board ship?

Yes, but here I have neither cards nor partners.

Oh, I play.

I myself pretend to play a good game.

Now we've got him. He won't move.

So Passepartout was sent for cards. Soon they were playing.

Soon they were crossing the plains which reach to the Atlantic Ocean. Suddenly, in the middle of nowhere, the train stopped.

See what is the matter.

You can't pass. The bridge at Medicine Bow is shaky. It could not take the weight of the train!

But the engineer spoke out.

Perhaps there is a way.

By putting on the highest speed, we might make it.

With the throttle wide open, traveling a hundred miles an hour, the train hardly ran on the rails at all.

The train seemed to leap from one side to the other. They had hardly crossed when the bridge, completely ruined, fell with a crash.

But more trouble was close at hand.

Why, you John Bull Englishman!

Pardon me, Mr. Fix. The fight is mine.

They decided to use guns to settle things.

The train will stop in Plum Creek for ten minutes. This shouldn't take long!

Very well!

Sorry, gentlemen. We're late and won't be stopping. Why not fight as we go along?

The rear car was cleared. The gentlemen would walk to each end, turn, and fire when the whistle blew.

Only in America can this happen!

Just at that moment, the train was attacked by a band of Sioux Indians.

It was a hard fight.

Unless the train is stopped, we are lost!

Stay, monsieur. I'll go.

The Fort Kearny station was an army post. If the train passed it, the Indians would probably kill them all.

Passepartout worked his way to the front end of the train.

He pulled the safety chain and unfastened the cars from the engine. It rushed ahead as the cars came to a stop.

Soldiers, hearing the shots, hurried up. The Indians rode off.

But three people had disappeared, among them Passepartout.

Are you going to chase the Indians?

Can I risk the lives of fifty to save three?

Would you leave those poor men to die? What about the one who saved our lives? I will go after him alone.

No sir, I'll send some good men with you.

When Phileas Fogg rode off after Passepartout, he knew he might lose his bet. Even one day's delay would keep him from his ship to Liverpool. But the safety of his servant came first.

Three hours later, the engine returned to pick up the cars and passengers.

Another train will be here tomorrow evening.

But that will be too late!

The train left. Evening came, and still they did not return. Aouda worried all through the long night.

But just after dawn, Fogg came riding back.

Meanwhile, during the night, Fix had met a man who could help them.

He has a sled with sails on it. When the wind is good, it fairly flies over the snow.

Indeed, these sleds could travel with the speed of a fast train.

By now the snow had hardened. With a good west wind, the sled's owner knew he could make a quick trip to Omaha. This was where trains to the East ran quite often.

They flew over the carpet of snow. Shortly before noon, Omaha was in sight.

We're there!

Fogg paid the man well, and they reached the station just in time to catch a train going east.

They changed trains in Chicago. Less than three days later the Hudson River and New York City came into view. Their train stopped right at the dock of the Cunard Steamship Line.

But the China for Liverpool had started three quarters of an hour before.

Since it was growing dark, Fogg took them to a hotel.

We shall find a ship to take tomorrow. Come!

Phileas Fogg slept soundly. When he left the hotel early the next morning, nine days, thirteen hours, and forty-five minutes remained.

I am Phileas Fogg of London. I see you are about to sail.

And I am Captain Andrew Speedy of Cardiff, bound for Bordeaux in an hour.

Have you any passengers?

I never have passengers. Too much in the way!

Will you carry me and three others to Liverpool?

No! I'm setting out for Bordeaux, and I shall go to Bordeaux!

With $8,000 to gain, Captain Speedy gave in. In less than an hour, Mr. Fogg's group was aboard.

And the Henrietta began her trip across the Atlantic.

Fogg locked Captain Speedy in his cabin. Fogg then paid the crew to let him steer the ship.

The passengers and crew alike were surprised that he knew so much about the sea.

But six days out, the engineer reported they were almost out of coal. Mr. Fogg thought for a while and then called the captain.

What's the matter? Where are we?

Seven hundred miles from Liverpool, and I must ask you to sell me this ship!

No, by all the devils, no!

But without coal we will have to burn it, piece by piece, to run the engine.

Here's sixty thousand dollars in American money. You may keep whatever we don't have to burn!

In a moment the captain forgot his anger. He even joined in sawing up the woodwork to keep the boilers at full steam.

You must understand. A bet of 20,000 pounds is at stake.

Well, Captain Fogg, you've got something of the Yankee about you.

Phileas Fogg at last reached Liverpool at twenty minutes before twelve on the twenty-first of December. He was only six hours from London by train.

Mr. Phileas Fogg, I arrest you in the Queen's name!

Fogg did not seem to worry about being in jail. He still had eight hours to reach the Reform Club.

Then, at thirty-five minutes past two...

Sir, forgive me. You looked like the bank robber I was searching for. But he was arrested three days ago. You are free!

Phileas Fogg looked Fix right in the eye. Then he made the only rapid motion he was ever known to make.

Fix got just what he deserved. Then Mr. Fogg and company left quickly for the station.

They had missed the afternoon express, but Mr. Fogg hired a special train on which they left at three o'clock.

The engineer was offered a great reward, but when they arrived in London, Mr. Fogg was five minutes late. He had lost the bet.

Fogg had spent a great deal of money on the trip. Now that he had lost the bet, he was ruined.

The next morning Mr. Fogg said that he would work all day. But in the evening he planned to speak with Aouda.

When I decided to bring you to Europe, I was rich. I planned to give you enough money to make you free and happy. Now I am ruined. But I would like to give you whatever I have left.

I don't need any money myself.

They say that two people can make a bitter life sweet.

They say so, yes.

Oh, Mr. Fogg! Do you want both a relative and a friend? Will you have me for a wife?

Yes, by heaven! I love you!

They called for Passe-partout. He understood at once, and with a great smile he began to prepare for a wedding which would take place the very next day.

Passepartout went out to buy what was needed. But in moments he was back.

You have made a mistake! We arrived a day early! We still have ten minutes left to win the bet!

Impossible!

But it was true. Traveling east around the world, they had gained an extra day. No one had thought about it until just then!

Well, gentlemen, I think we have won the bet!

Don't let us be too quick. You know Mr. Fogg never arrives too soon or too late.

Here I am, gentlemen.

So the bet was won, and our story ends. Of the 20,000 pounds, only a thousand were left after their expenses. This he divided between Passepartout and Detective Fix, with whom he was not really angry. And Fogg? He had gained a beautiful wife!

The End